The Borderlands

By Neil Stevenson

A story written for Angelica and Tamsin

Chapter One

For as long as anyone could remember, the neighbouring Kingdoms of Zumbovia and Maduria had lived happily side-by-side. But this is the story of how the two countries were brought to the brink of war, by a wicked father and his son. It is also a story of courage, of love, and of good triumphing over evil.

The two Kingdoms were separated by high, wooded hills that were astonishingly beautiful. They were not often visited, and most people stuck to the track-way that linked Madovar and Zumborg, the two capital cities. The border between the Kingdoms was poorly defined, and not at all easy to follow. Both countries simply referred to the whole area of hills as The Borderlands.

One day, King Otto of Zumbovia gave orders for a routine border patrol to be made. He had no way of knowing that a Princess, from neighbouring Maduria, had just set off to visit the same area of The Borderlands.

The Princess was called Emelia, the only daughter of King Leopold and Queen Helena. Sadly, the King had died when Emelia had been a baby, leaving the Queen to single-handedly raise their only heir to the throne. With her long, chestnut brown hair, tanned skin and piercing blue-green eyes, Emelia was indeed beautiful. But she was also intelligent, and she had an infectious laugh that most men found irresistible. Hardly surprising then, that suitors had started to visit the palace, seeking her hand in marriage. There'd been just a few at first, but then they'd started coming much more often. This might have been fine, had any of them been remotely likeable, but unfortunately none had. You name it - rude, arrogant, boring, ugly, unintelligent, smelly-breathed - she'd seen them all, and more besides.

Emelia didn't even feel ready for marriage. But seeing as she was the last of the family line, the Queen was keen for her to marry young, and to have lots of children. Emelia wanted to experience more of the world around her before taking on these royal responsibilities. She had particularly wanted to experience the natural beauty of The Borderlands for herself, and seeing it as a chance to get away from the palace for a while, she had asked her mother for permission to go. At first the Queen had said no, but after weeks of nagging, she had finally consented, on condition that six soldiers from the elite State Guard accompany her. Johnson, the Princess' private butler, would also travel with her.

The Zumbovian border patrol consisted of twelve cavalry soldiers on horseback, led by the Kings' nephew Torrian. He was a dark and towering figure of a man, and feared by all who served under him. Torrian usually led these occasional patrols, although he regarded them purely as an opportunity to restock his larder with deer, wild boar, and in fact any poor creature who had the bad luck to meet with his dreaded crossbow. Torrian was a power-hungry and ruthless man and, like his father The Duke, he was well known for his bad moods and cruel behaviour. The Dukes' brother, King Otto, had never married, and he was unhappy that The Duke, and Torrian after him, were next in line for the throne.

Chapter Two

As both parties made their way into the hills, Torrian with his horsemen, and Emelia with Johnson and the State Guards, neither knew of the other. So of course when they met, it came as something of a surprise. It happened in a wooded valley, beside a beautiful lake. Large fish were quite easily visible; swimming lazily in the deep, clear waters. Emelia had discovered the lake quite by chance, and had immediately decided that they should camp there for the night. The Guards set about erecting tents and getting a campfire established, while Johnson prepared supper for everyone. Emelia wandered to one end of the lake, where a grassy slope, rich with pretty meadow flowers and wild orchids, sloped gently down to a small beach.

She had only been there for a moment, when a sudden cracking sound came from close within the forest, and Emelia spun around, startled. A deer ran out into open ground, across the grass, and straight past her, before disappearing into the woods beyond. Then came more crashing, and the galloping of hooves. Torrian came bursting from the trees, bringing his huge horse to a halt directly in front of Emelia. His horsemen followed, close behind.

"Where'd it go?" he bellowed at the startled Princess.

"You mean that deer?" She asked.

"Of course I mean the deer, you foolish girl!" he shouted, "Tell me where it went, and quickly, before it gets away!"

"Firstly, I am not a fool," she said calmly, "and secondly, I rather hope that it does get away. From you, that is."

Torrian leapt down from his horse, and strode angrily towards the Princess, saying "You? Dare to defy..."

But then his eyes studied her for the first time, and he found himself gazing upon quite the loveliest woman he'd ever met. Of course he had no idea who she was. He was also unaware, that in the excitement of chasing the deer, he had in fact strayed across the border, and on to Madurian soil. He slowed, and then stopped before her, mouth gaping.

"You may wish to close your mouth, sire," said Emelia, a smile playing across her face. "There are insects about."

Torrian snapped his mouth closed angrily, and then barked, "You dare to insult me! You obviously have no idea to whom you speak!"

"You're correct," the Princess replied, "I have no idea. Nor, I think, do I wish to."

"Well you're about to learn," Torrian growled, and then yelled to his men, "Seize her!"

As two men grabbed Emelia, her screams alerted Johnson, who looked up in time to see her being dragged up on to a horse. He also recognised the unmistakable form of Torrian, who he'd seen at a royal function some years earlier. He turned and shouted to the State Guards, but already Torrian and his men were disappearing into the forest. The Guards gave chase, but Torrian and his patrol knew the hills well, and gave them the slip easily, getting away with the Princess as their captive.

Chapter Three

One of the State Guards returned immediately to Madovar, and informed Queen Helena of what had happened. She slumped into her throne, and burst into tears. It was several moments before she spoke.

With a tremor in her voice, she said, "Torrian! I've never liked him, but what's he *thinking* of, kidnapping my daughter? Has he gone insane? Order my Ambassador to set off for Zumbovia straight away, and to demand her immediate release!"

The Ambassador set off without delay, but it took him several days to reach Zumborg. He sought an audience with King Otto as soon as he arrived. Of course the King knew nothing of the kidnapping, and he found it hard to believe that Torrian was capable of such a thing. But Torrian had in fact taken the Princess to where he lived – a dark and imposing fortress called Castle Suvorov, which was more than a days' ride from the capital. The Ambassador requested that the King send some men to question Torrian, but Otto refused. He also refused permission for the Ambassador to visit

Castle Suvorov personally, and so he had no choice but to return to Madovar without the Princess.

Meanwhile Emelia found herself brought before Torrian, who announced that she was to become his wife. The Princess was horrified, and said that she'd rather die than marry such an ogre. Torrian had her locked up, high in one of the dark towers of the castle, telling her that she'd remain there until she changed her mind. So there she stayed, alone except for a kindly maid called Sophie, who brought her food and drink three times a day. Of course neither Sophie nor Torrian knew that the prisoner was the Madurian Princess, and had no idea of the trouble that her kidnapping was beginning to cause between the two countries.

Queen Helena was dismayed when the Ambassador returned without her daughter. She sent him straight back to Zumborg again, with a stark message for King Otto: If the Ambassador returned empty-handed a second time, then the entire Zumbovian army would come to get her. This time, the Ambassador took a homing-falcon with him, a bird that, if needed, could carry a message back to the Queen very quickly. Three days later, when the Ambassador delivered the Queens' message to Otto, the King became very alarmed, and ordered a trusted manservant to ride immediately to Castle Suvorov.

Chapter Four

A week had now passed since Torrian had kidnapped the Princess. Each morning Torrian had Emelia brought before him, and each day he demanded that she marry him, and each day she made it quite clear that she never would. On the seventh day she told him, "I'd never marry you, not if you were the last man on earth! When, I wonder, will you get this into your thick head?" This had made Torrian furious, and once again he'd sent her back to the tower.

After she'd gone, he muttered, "I've had enough of this. If she refuses me again tomorrow, I'll kill her myself!" Sophie, the maid, overheard what he'd said, and became very frightened for Emelias' safety. She decided that despite the danger to herself, she would have to help the girl to escape. That night Sophie crept up into the tower, and unlocked the door. She woke Emelia up, and explained what she'd heard Torrian say. Then she helped the Princess to dress as a servant-girl, and the two of them crept quietly out of the castle, and down to the village, where Sophies' brother Ivan had a cottage.

In the morning, when Torrian demanded that his prisoner be once again brought before him, the guards returned fearfully, with news that she had disappeared. Torrian flew into a rage, and ordered that the entire castle be searched. Of course she wasn't found. Torrian clenched his fists and roared, "Search the village! The countryside! Everywhere! I want that girl back here *immediately!* Send out all of my men! Every single one!"

At Ivans' cottage, Emelia was already awake, and Sophie had given her some breakfast. After she'd eaten, she said, "I have to tell you both something, but you must promise to tell nobody else."

Ivan and Sophie nodded, and the Princess told them who she was. They were shocked, and Ivan was particularly afraid of what Torrian would do to the three of them, if they were caught. He knew that he had to get the Princess away from the village at all costs, and to help her get back to the safety of her own country as soon as possible. But Ivan didn't know The Borderlands at all well, and he realised that Emelia would need an experienced guide to show her the way. He immediately thought of a woodsman called Josef, who lived alone in a round-house, deep in the forest. Josef knew The Borderlands like the back of his own hands, and only came to the village when he needed to. He much preferred the solitude of the woods. Ivan decided to take the Princess to him. Tearfully the Princess and Sophie said goodbye, promising that one day they would meet again. Then without further delay, Ivan and Emelia set off.

Torrian was still in the foulest of moods when King Ottos' manservant arrived an hour later. He was shocked to learn that it was the Madurian Princess he'd kidnapped. But rather than admit to what he'd done, and then have to explain how she'd now disappeared, he found it far easier to lie, and simply said, "Me? Kidnap a Princess? How ridiculous! I've no idea what you're talking about!"

And so the manservant returned to Zumborg, but it would be evening before he arrived there. As he passed through the village, he couldn't help but notice a great many of Torrians' horsemen about. They had just finished searching every house, and having found no trace of the Princess, were preparing to widen the search to the surrounding countryside.

Chapter Five

Emelia and Ivan had paused to drink water at a spring, when they heard horsemen approaching. Quickly they crept into the undergrowth and hid, hardly daring to breathe. Five of Torrians' men pulled up, allowing their horses to drink. Suddenly one of the men shouted out, and held up something pink. Emelia gasped – it was a ribbon from her hair. The other men gathered around and spoke briefly, and then quickly remounted their horses and galloped further into the forest.

"They'll certainly go as far as Josefs' place," Ivan whispered, "but then they'll most probably come back this way. We have to carry on, so let's hope that we can hide from them when they come back."

But the horsemen did not return, and by evening Emelia and Ivan had almost reached the glade where Josef lived. Ivan feared that Torrians' men would be there, but as they crept towards the edge of the woods, all seemed peaceful. There was no sign of movement at the round-house, although a gentle curl of smoke rose from the chimney.

"He's home at least," Ivan whispered.
Then a voice spoke, straight into their ears, "No he's not, he's right behind you!"

Ivan and Emelia jumped, and spun around. Before them was a tall man who might have been handsome, were it not for the mud smeared across his face, and the clothing he wore, which appeared to be made entirely of leaves.

"Princess Emelia, I presume?" said the man, bowing to her.
"I – I am!" said the Princess, gathering her composure a little.
"And do I assume that you are Josef?"
"Indeed so, your Highness. And do *I* assume that *you* are in trouble?"
"I must get home to Maduria, and I understand that you can take me there. My mother, the Queen, will pay you well if you do."
"I will certainly take you, but we must wait until morning."
Then Ivan spoke. "Have you seen any of Torrians' men?"
"Five of them came here this afternoon," said Josef. "I sent them up towards Wilderness Mountain. That's a place even I won't go without very good reason. By now they will certainly be lost, and quite probably fending off the hungry, wild

animals that live up there. Either that or wallowing in quick-sand!"

The Princess smiled. Already she liked this softly spoken man of the woods.

"Now," said Josef, "We should eat. And then you two should sleep. I'll keep guard outside tonight, just in case."

Chapter Six

King Ottos' manservant returned from Castle Suvorov, galloping across the drawbridge and into the palace courtyard. King Otto and Queen Helenas' Ambassador were waiting for him.

"Well?" asked the King.

"Torrian says that he hasn't seen the Princess, your Majesty," said the manservant breathlessly.

"And did you believe him?"

"I'm afraid that I did not, sire. Everyone in the castle seemed extremely nervous, and a great many horsemen were about in the village. Torrian himself seemed even angrier than usual."

"What are you going to do, your Majesty?" asked the Ambassador.

"What *can* I do? I've no proof that he's holding your Princess. And I can hardly unleash the army upon my brothers' only son without proof. Torrian is second in line to the throne!"

"I doubt that my Queen will see it that way," said the Ambassador firmly, turning towards the door.

The Ambassador went quickly upstairs to his room, where he wrote a hurried message on a tiny scroll. Attaching it to the homing-falcons' leg, he took the bird to the window and set it free. He watched it wheel around the palace courtyard a few times, and then fly away in the direction of The Borderlands, and the Kingdom of Maduria beyond. The bird arrived at Madovar in the small hours, and by sunrise Queen Helena had ordered her entire army to march on Zumbovia.

Emelia emerged from the round-house, having slept surprisingly well. A mist had formed in the glade overnight, and shafts of sunlight were shining through it. Josef stood before her, now clean, shaven, and rather more conventionally clothed. His long blonde hair was tied back in a pony-tail, and she was surprised at how handsome he was. The Princess was momentarily lost for words, and she blushed slightly.

"We should leave at once, your Highness," he said, and the Princess nodded. She turned to Ivan, hugged him, and said goodbye. As Ivan headed back towards the village, Josef and Emelia set off in the opposite direction, towards the foot-hills of The Borderlands.

Torrian sat fuming in the court-room of Castle Suvorov. A day had now passed since the girl had escaped, and the shock of who she really was, had begun to sink in. All except five of his horsemen had returned from searching the countryside, and none of them had any news of her whereabouts. She seemed to have vanished into thin air. He was just wondering how things could get any worse, when a servant came in nervously, and cowered before him.

"What d'you want?" he barked.
"It's your father, the Duke, sire. He's here to see you."

Now it will come as no surprise to hear that the Duke was every bit as nasty and treacherous as Torrian himself. In fact Torrian might best be described as being a chip off the old block. But there was little doubt in Torrians' mind, why his father was now visiting. To arrive so early in the morning, meant that he had travelled to Castle Suvorov throughout the night. Torrian glanced worriedly at the door, and bellowed, "Great! That's *all* I need! Well - you'd better show him in!"

Minutes later the Duke strode in, and Torrian walked towards him, forcing a smile and opening his arms to embrace.

"Father! What an unexpected surprise! You must be hungry. I'll have breakfast brought..."

"Never mind breakfast!" hissed the Duke, "King Otto summoned me to the palace last night. He seems to think that you've kidnapped Princess Emelia of Maduria! Tell me it's not true!"

Torrian gulped, and then said, "I – I'm sorry father, but it is."

"You stupid fool!" spat the Duke. "What were you thinking of? Idiot! Have you any idea what trouble you've caused? And anyway, where is she now?"

"I- I don't know, father. She escaped, yesterday. But I didn't know she was a Princess when I..."

"Be *quiet!*" the Duke hissed, "I need to think. I need to find a way out of this mess! And you'd better pray that I do, otherwise you'll find yourself spending the rest of your days in one of the dungeons under Zumborg Palace!"

Chapter Seven

Josef had decided to follow a little-known trail to Maduria, which passed up through the rocky peaks of the highest hills in The Borderland, through an area known as The Pinnacles. He had told Emelia that the path would eventually rejoin the main track-way between the capitals, but not until after they had crossed the border, and it would take them a day longer than the conventional route. Josef felt sure that Torrian would expect the Princess to take the easiest, quickest route back to Maduria, and would be unlikely to search The Pinnacles. As Josef and Emelia followed the rocky trail upwards, they were relaxed and spoke easily with one another. Emelia had already insisted that he call her by her first name. At particularly steep parts of the path, Josef held her hand to steady her, and she found this so agreeable that she looked forward to other difficult parts of the path, so that she may hold it again. Josef, who had lived most of his life alone in the woods, had never met so beautiful a woman, and was quite overwhelmed to be alone with her. However, he was also acutely aware that a Princess could never be interested in a simple woodsman such as himself.

Chapter Eight

The Duke had been pacing up and down in the Court-Room of Castle Suvorov for several hours. Torrian had crept out, but he quickly returned when his father began yelling for him.

"Torrian! About time! I have an idea, which might just save your neck! It's the only way, so you'd better pray that it works!"

"What is it, father?" Torrian asked.

"It's beautifully simple. We'll blame it all on King Otto! If we can make the Madurian troops think that the King is holding the Princess, then they'll be sure to attack his palace. When they don't find the Princess there, they will certainly take the King prisoner, and possibly even take him back to Madovar. And then, dear boy, the throne will be ours!"

Torrian smiled for the first time in more than a day. But it was an evil, chilling smile. Then he said, "So how do we do that, father?"

The Duke sent for two scrolls, and wrote hastily on each one. He signed both, and then sealed them by pressing his cygnet ring into blobs of melted wax. Two riders were despatched, each carrying a scroll. The first rode towards Zumborg, under strict instructions to give the scroll to none other than the King. The second rider headed towards The Borderlands, his scroll addressed to the Commander-in-Chief of the advancing Madurian army.

By the end of the day, Josef and Emelia had reached the top of a steep pass, between two of the highest Pinnacles. The view was breath taking, and the two sat watching the sun setting, hands held, but not speaking. It grew chilly, and Josef produced a thick blanket that he draped around both of them. Emelia kissed him on the cheek, and then rested her head on his shoulder. She soon fell asleep. Josef on the other hand, who had never been kissed by anybody in his life before, let alone by a beautiful Princess, did not sleep a wink.

Some hours after nightfall, the first scroll was delivered to the palace in Zumborg. As ordered, the rider placed it directly into the hands of King Otto, who read it immediately:

My Brother,

I rode all night, and I reached Castle Suvorov by daybreak. I have questioned Torrian at length, and I'm certain that he hasn't even seen the Princess, let alone kidnapped her. We have made a thorough search of the entire castle, grounds, and even far out into the surrounding countryside, but we've found no trace of her. I can only conclude that she is not in this part of Zumbovia, and that the allegations made against my son are the result of a dreadful mistake. Accordingly my son and I will travel to Zumborg tomorrow, and we'll be glad to help you sort out this terrible misunderstanding.

Yours sincerely,

Your brother, the Duke

The King put the scroll down, wondering what to make of it. He decided to show it to Queen Helenas' Ambassador, and sent a servant to fetch him. The Ambassador duly appeared, read the scroll carefully, and then said, "The trouble is that Princess Emelias' private butler *saw* Torrian take her. Johnson is absolutely trustworthy. So I'm afraid, Your Highness, that you must ask yourself how much you trust the Duke and his son."

"Well I..." began the King, but then he realised just how little he *did* trust them.

"I think," said the Ambassador, "that there's very little more I can do here, and under the circumstances it's better that I leave. I'll head off back to Maduria at first light."

Early the following morning, as the Ambassador galloped away from Zumborg, the second scroll was delivered to the Commander-in-Chief of the Madurian army. They had made a camp in the heart of The Borderlands, less than two days' march from Zumbovian capital. The Commander read the scroll with a startled expression on his face:

To the Commander-in-Chief
Madurian Army

Sire,

I was greatly concerned when I learned that your Princess had gone missing, and am most worried that my son Torrian stands wrongly accused of her disappearance. I have come to my sons' castle, and I have personally organised a thorough search of the castle and surrounding country. I must assure you that she is not here, nor has she ever been, and that my son is entirely innocent.

Furthermore, I have to tell you that a trusted servant of mine saw a girl answering to your Princess' description, being escorted into King Ottos' palace in Zumborg, not two days ago. It saddens me to say that all evidence seems to point at my brother the King. He is unhappy with the idea of me succeeding him to the throne, and I feel that he'll do anything to prevent it happening. I therefore urge you to march immediately to Zumborg, where I am certain that you will find your Princess, languishing in one of King Ottos' many dungeons.

Yours faithfully,

The Duke of Zumbovia

The Commander-in-Chief looked up from the scroll, and then gave an order to strike camp, and to begin the march towards Zumborg. He also despatched a rider to take the scroll back to Queen Helena in Madovar.

Chapter Nine

Princess Emelia had awoken to find herself still wrapped in the blanket, with Josef sitting nearby, making tea over a small fire. After a simple breakfast of bread and ham, they spent the morning walking through the highest, sharpest peaks of The Pinnacles. Josef was still floating on a cloud since the goodnight kiss, although he was far too shy to say anything. But the way Emelia looked at him, the way she smiled, the easy way in which she spoke with him, even though it was ridiculous to even think that she might actually like him, he couldn't help how he felt. He was falling hopelessly in love with her.

Emelia too, was lost in thought. She knew that her swift return to Madovar was highly important, but part of her wanted this mountainous walk with Josef to never end. She'd never met a man like him before. Not only strong, and handsome, but so much more real than the endless stream of unbearable suitors that she'd endured at the palace. But what on earth would her mother say, if she brought home a common woodsman?

Meanwhile on the main track-way between the capitals, while the Madurian army had stopped for lunch, the Ambassador galloped into their encampment and dismounted from his horse. Both he and the Commander-in-Chief were a little confused when they learned what had been written in the scrolls they hadn't already seen.

"They don't make sense! In fact the whole thing sounds rather fishy to me," said the Ambassador, "I wouldn't trust the Duke or his son as far as I could throw them!"

The Commander-in-Chief agreed, and said, "We'd certainly be foolish to attack King Ottos' palace on their say-so. I've sent the scroll to the Queen, with my fastest rider. I hope that she'll know what to do."

Queen Helena was at lunch, although in fact she was deep in thought, and toying with her food. Suddenly a servant burst in, and walked briskly towards her.

"My apologies ma'am, but I thought you would want to see this right away." It was of course the scroll, just delivered by the Commander-in-Chiefs' horseman. She read it twice, and then frowned. Eventually she asked for Johnson to be brought to her, and he appeared minutes later.

"Read this, Johnson," said the Queen, and tell me what you think."

Johnson read the scroll carefully, and then said, "I simply cannot believe a word of it, ma'am. It's astonishing! I saw Torrian capture the Princess with my own eyes. I fear that he and his father are trying to trick us into attacking King Otto. After all, if anything happens to the King, we both know who stands to gain the most."

"I agree entirely, Johnson. In fact I believe that King Otto is in great danger. I must deal with this personally. I want my fastest four-horse coach made ready as soon as possible. And I want you to come with me."

Chapter Ten

By the middle of the afternoon, as the Queen and Johnson were speeding away from Madovar, the Princess and Josef were descending from The Pinnacles. Earlier, from one final spectacular viewpoint, Josef had pointed out the main trackway leading between the two Kingdoms, threading its' way between low foothills in the distance. The two of them would join it for the final part of their journey to Madovar. Both of them were privately thinking of how their time alone was growing short. Josef desperately wanted to tell Emelia how he felt about her, but he was simply too shy.

They had clambered down a steep-sided valley, following a small river that was tumbling in a succession of pretty waterfalls. They eventually came upon a huge cascade, plunging into a crystal clear pool. It was a beautiful place, surrounded by vivid green ferns and mosses. They stopped to drink, and to rest. Josef realised that this might be his last chance to tell Emelia of how he felt.

She must have read his mind, because she smiled, and said, "You like me, don't you Josef?"

He looked up, surprised, and then he smiled too, but nervously.

Then she said, "I like you too, you know."

"Really?" said Josef, as she stepped slowly towards him.

"Really!" she said softly, and then she kissed him gently on his lips. Gently, they put their arms around each other, and kissed again.

Chapter Eleven

Torrian and his father were drinking beer together in the Court-Room of Castle Suvorov. They clinked their goblets, and the Duke spoke with smug satisfaction.

"Well, my boy," he said, "it seems that we've turned a difficult problem to our advantage! If all goes to plan, Queen Helenas' army will attack Otto in the morning, and by the evening I'll be sitting on the throne! I'm setting off for Zumborg early tomorrow, and of course you must accompany me. You wouldn't want to miss my hour of glory now, would you?"

"Not for the world, father," replied Torrian, with relish.

As the two of them drank ale and dreamed of how rich and powerful they were about to become, Princess Emelia and Josef resumed their journey down from The Pinnacles, into the low foothills of The Borderlands. It was easy walking now, and it wasn't long before they reached the main track-way between Zumbovia and Maduria. They paused briefly to drink from a stream, and then headed in the direction of Madovar. Only a few minutes had passed, when Josef noticed a carriage racing towards them, its' four horses galloping at full speed.

"That's my mothers' carriage!" Emelia exclaimed, immediately letting go of Josefs' hand.
"You mean, your mother the Queen?" Josef said, a little nervously. "Do you think she's in it?"
"We're about to find out, Josef! She would only be going to Zumborg if something really bad has happened."

As the carriage approached, Emelia stood in the middle of the track-way, and waved for it to stop. She had forgotten that she was dressed as a servant-girl, with clothes now dirty from several days' travelling. The coachman yelled at her to move aside. Emelia ran up on to the bank, and the carriage sped past, without slowing at all. Through an open window she saw the Queen for a moment, and she shouted, "Mother! Stop!"

For several seconds the carriage continued at speed, but then the coachman pulled hard on the reins, and brought it to a halt. He jumped down, opened the carriage door, and out stepped the Queen. Emelia ran to her, and the two of them hugged tightly.

"My daughter!" sobbed Queen Helena. "Thank the heavens that you're safe! But why are you here? And dressed in such filthy rags!"

"Oh mother, I was kidnapped by a man named Torrian, but I was able to escape. These clothes are to disguise me."

"And who's this you're with?" asked the Queen, gesturing to Josef, who had approached them.

"This is Josef, mother. He's been showing me the way. Without him, I'd hate to think where I would be now."

Josef bowed, and said, "At your service ma'am."

"I owe you a debt of gratitude Josef," the Queen said. "But many things have happened while you've been missing, and it's most important that I get to Zumborg as soon as I can. Both of you, get in the carriage, and I'll tell you everything on the way."

Chapter Twelve

The Madurian army had continued to march all afternoon, and by evening had come to within a few miles of Zumborg, where the Commander-in-Chief had ordered them to make camp for the night. It was here that the Queens' carriage caught up with them, pulling into the encampment some hours after darkness.

"Your Majesty!" the Commander-in-Chief said, bowing deeply. "I'm so glad you are here, madam. I was unsure what I should do next."

"Don't worry, I have a plan," the Queen said, "but first I must speak with King Otto personally. Have fresh horses hitched to my carriage right away. There isn't a moment to lose!"

"Is that wise, your Majesty?" asked the Commander cautiously. "After all, the King is accused of kidnapping your daughter. If you show up, who knows what he'll do to you?"

"Otto is innocent, I'm convinced of it," said the Queen. "Now, please hurry up and change these horses!"

After a few minutes the Queen, Princess Emelia and Josef departed for Zumborg. They arrived at the palace shortly before midnight, and were shown immediately in to see the King, who was dressed in his pyjamas.

"My lady!" King Otto exclaimed. Then he saw Emelia, and said, "Princess! Thank the heavens! You're safe! I can't tell you how relieved I am to see you!"

"Otto," said the Queen, handing him the scroll, "You need to read this."

King Otto read what the Duke had written to the Commander-in-Chief, and then sat heavily into his throne, looking visibly shocked.

"That scheming, evil brother of mine!" he said eventually, "So he's behind all of this!"

"No, your Majesty," said Emelia, stepping forward. "It was Torrian who kidnapped me. The Duke has seen it as a chance to blame you, and seize the throne."

"I'll have them both clapped in irons!" the King said firmly. "When they get here tomorrow, I'll have them arrested on sight!"

"There's one small problem with that, Otto," said the Queen. "Torrian and the Duke will be expecting to see my army in charge of your castle, and if they don't, they may easily escape into the forest."

"Quite right, Helena," the King said thoughtfully. "What should we do?"

"I have an idea," said the Queen, "My army is camped just a few miles outside the city. I suggest that we station some of my soldiers at the city gates, and more on the palace walls. In fact we should have them anywhere in the city where they can easily be seen. It would make the Duke and Torrian *think* that my army has captured Zumborg. They will assume that you, Otto, have been arrested for kidnapping Emelia, and with any luck we'll capture them both easily."

The King agreed to the plan, and by morning everyone was in place.

Chapter Thirteen

It was early in the afternoon. Torrian and The Duke had been riding constantly since first light, and had reached a place where the forest ended abruptly at a cliff. Dismounting, Torrian produced a telescope, and crept towards the edge. Spread out below him was the entire city of Zumborg. He spied out across the city for a few moments, and then turned to his father, his grin never more sinister.

"The City has been captured, father!" he said, jubilantly. "Even the Madurian flag is flying from the palace!"
"Excellent!" said the Duke, rubbing his hands. "You are looking at the next King of Zumbovia! Come on, dear boy, we have a throne to claim!"

They descended by way of a steep pathway, and approached the city gates, where a number of Madurian soldiers were stationed. When the soldiers saw the Duke and Torrian, they stood to attention and saluted them. They had been given strict instructions by the Queen to do this. As the two rode on into the city, other groups of Madurian soldiers showed similar respect. They reached the palace, and rode straight into the main courtyard, where the Commander-in-Chief was waiting for them.

"Your Highness," he said, "Thank you for the scroll you sent me, sir. As you can see, I have done exactly what you suggested. We have arrested the King, and we are holding him for you."

"Take me to him!" barked the Duke.

The Commander led the Duke and Torrian up to the State Room, which was lined down both sides by Madurian troops, all standing to attention. At the far end of the room King Otto was sitting on his throne.

"You can get off there, for a start!" the Duke yelled, striding forwards.

"That's no way to greet your brother!" the King said, not moving.

Torrian immediately suspected that something was wrong. He backed away to the door, but found to his alarm that it had been closed and locked behind them. The Duke suspected nothing, and addressing the Madurian guards he said, "Take Otto away and throw him in a dungeon! I have no desire to see this *kidnapper* ever again!"

The soldiers moved swiftly forward, and before the Duke had a chance to move, he had a dozen Madurian swords all pointing directly at him. When the King spoke, there was a real sadness in his voice, "My own brother, that you would betray me, and tell such lies about me, I can hardly believe what you have done."

Queen Helena and Princess Emelia stepped out from behind a long tapestry, where they had been hiding. Torrian gasped, and looked around like a trapped animal. But as yet, the Madurian soldiers had overlooked him, and he crept quietly behind another of the tapestries.

The Queen approached the Duke and said, "The game's up, I'm afraid. You've been found out! Both you, and your despicable son!"

Emelia suddenly realised that she couldn't see Torrian anywhere. She wished that Josef was there with her, but as a commoner he hadn't been permitted into the State Room.

A moment later her hair was grabbed from behind, pulling her head back, and she felt the cold steel of a dagger against her throat.

"One move and she's dead!" Torrian spat. He dragged the Princess towards the doors, yelling for them to be unlocked. There was no choice but to open them, and in a moment they were both gone.

Out in the courtyard there now stood a prison-wagon. It had been brought there to take the Duke and Torrian away. Torrian quickly bundled the Princess inside, locked the bolts, climbed aboard, and rode out of the palace. He was wondering how on earth he was going to get past the many Madurian soldiers in the city, and at the gates. Unfortunately they were still under orders to stand to attention and salute, if they saw either the Duke, or his son. This is exactly what they did, as Torrian raced out of the city, and up into the forest beyond.

Chapter Fourteen

The Queen collapsed with shock, and King Otto ran to assist her. The Commander-in-Chief was left wondering how on earth so many soldiers had overlooked Torrian, and immediately ordered his soldiers to give chase. They returned an hour later, with news that the prison-wagon had been discovered abandoned, a couple of miles into the forest. King Otto called a meeting, and they discussed what course of action they should take.

"We have not one, but *two* armies at our disposal," He said, " Surely we can locate one single man, however big the forest is!"

"It's not that simple Sire," said the Kings' Chief Advisor. "Torrian knows the forest like nobody else, and even if we manage to corner him, who knows what he'll do to the Princess?"

"There must be something we can do!" said the King, exasperated.

"I can help," said a quiet voice from the back of the room.

The King looked up and said, "Step forward, whoever you are, and pray tell me what you can do, that two armies cannot!"

It was Josef who emerged from the shadows. "Your Majesty, my name is Josef, and I have lived in the forest for my whole life. Nobody knows it better than I, my Lord. I can track Torrian, and I can catch him too."

"A bold claim indeed!" said the King. "You may join in the search, and I'm sure that your skills will be useful!"

"With respect, your Majesty," Josef said, bowing slightly, "I cannot *join in* any search. I can only do it alone. The noise your soldiers make would certainly alert Torrian to our presence, and their boots would destroy the clues I can use to track him."

"Are you seriously suggesting that I entrust the rescue of the Princess to one man?" the King asked, incredulously.

"I trust him," said a woman's voice, and Queen Helena stepped forward. After collapsing, she had been carried to a nearby chamber, where the Kings' physicians had attended to her. Although still feeling shaky, she had returned to see what was happening. "This man," she continued, "has rescued my daughter once, and I see no reason why he shouldn't rescue her again!"

"Very well," said the King, and then to Josef he said, "What do you need?"

"Simply to be taken to the prison-wagon, Sire. And then left there, alone."

Less than an hour later, Josef was standing beside the empty prison-wagon, with the rattle of the cart that had brought him there, receding into the distance. He was once again disguised in leaves and mud, and almost invisible, except for when he moved.

Having lived in the forest for his entire life, Josef was an expert at tracking animals, using the signs that they left behind them – footprints, broken twigs, grass brushed aside, leaves snapped from plants, and so on – but he had never used his skills to track a man before. He picked up the trail easily, and before long he was making his way quickly and silently into the depths of the forest. It was close to nightfall.

Torrian had forced Emelia to walk at knife-point for several miles into the forest, until it was too dark to go any further. Then he had tied the Princess to a tree, at the edge of a small clearing. Pressing the blade of the knife against her cheek, he menacingly whispered in her ear, "If you make a single noise, I will kill you immediately. Do you understand, *Princess?*"

Chapter Fifteen

During the night a light rain had begun falling, and by daybreak the Princess and Torrian were soaked to the skin. Neither had slept much. Emelia had been too frightened, and Torrian had been nervously listening out for any unusual sounds. He hadn't heard anything, and so he was pretty relaxed as he wandered a few feet into the forest to have a wee. A slight movement in the forest ahead of him suddenly caught his attention. What he saw, or thought he saw, made him shake his head in disbelief. Had that really been a man, made entirely of leaves, dart from behind one tree trunk to another? He shook his head again, his breath and heartbeat quickening.

Torrian drew his sword. He stared at where the figure had been, but nothing stirred. He wheeled about, scanning the foliage, but all he saw was the Princess, still tied to a tree. She was smiling at him, and she said, "You're really in trouble now!" "Shut up!" Torrian hissed, and he turned back, looking at where he'd seen the leaf-man. He could see nothing but trees. A sudden rustling sound to Torrians' left made him jump, but again he could see nothing. Then the crack of a branch to his right startled him, and he spun around. This time he could see the leaf-man again, quite clearly this time, stood facing him, not very far away. Torrian charged towards him, sword at the ready. The leaf-man didn't move, but he appeared to be holding a rope that extended up into the canopy of trees. As Torrian ran forwards, the leaf-man let go of the rope, which immediately started to shoot upwards. Suddenly Torrian became aware of the four corners of a net lifting up from the ground around him, and a moment later he was trapped in it, flying upwards. He struggled, but it was useless. He was caught, suspended high above where he'd been a moment earlier.

The leaf-man walked calmly underneath him, looked up, and said "Hang on a minute," before continuing to where the Princess lay. Powerless to do anything, Torrian watched as the leaf-man cut the ropes tying her hands, and helped her gently to her feet. Then, to his astonishment, the two embraced, and kissed each other several times.

Then, with the agility of a monkey, the leaf-man quickly climbed the tree from which Torrian was hanging, and out on to a thick branch, bringing the two face to face.
"Who are you?" snarled Torrian furiously.

"Just a common woodsman, most of the time. But every now and again I rescue a beautiful princess, and deliver her from the clutches of an evil, tyrannical monster!"

"I'll kill you with my bare hands, so I will!" Torrian roared.

Josef reached out, grabbing the net, and set Torrian spinning around slowly. "Look around you, Torrian. Do you see anyone coming to your rescue? Your father would, but unfortunately he's already locked in a dungeon! And there's nobody else who would come for you, is there? Face it Torrian, you're finished!"

Torrian was speechless with rage, and all he could do was growl, and spin slowly.

Josef climbed down from the tree, took Emelias' hand, and the two of them set off into the forest, towards Zumborg. Once Torrian realised that they were leaving, he began to shout at them.

"Hey!" he yelled, "You aren't going to leave me up here, are you?"

"Only for tonight!" Josef called back to him. "We'll send some soldiers to fetch you tomorrow. With luck, they might even find you!"

"*Come back!*" Torrian screamed. "Let me *down!* I'll pay you! *Anything!*" He continued to shout until the two were way beyond earshot.

Emelia and Josef reached the city by late afternoon. Emelia was cold and utterly exhausted, and Josef had carried her for the last few miles. Guards at the city gates saw them approaching, and immediately sent out a carriage, which took them to the palace. King Otto and Queen Helena were overjoyed to see them.

Chapter Sixteen

At first light, a Detachment of soldiers had been sent to collect Torrian. He'd been hanging in the tree all night, and it had begun to rain again shortly after midnight. He'd roared and screamed himself hoarse, and then from sheer exhaustion, he'd slept for an hour. He was cold, wet, and miserable. There was no anger left in him. When the soldiers lowered him to the ground, he just quietly held out his arms for the handcuffs to be fitted. He was carted off unceremoniously, and thrown into the same dungeon as his father, where they both remained, bickering and arguing incessantly, until the Grand Court Hearing, several weeks later.

When Princess Emelia awoke, the sun was already high in the sky. She felt very much better. And she was safe again! Her first thought was to find Josef. The mere thought of him made her heart swell. She quickly dressed and went in search of him.

Josef had in fact been up for several hours. Queen Helena arrived to see him.

"Dear Josef," she said, "My country and I, in fact I more than anybody, owe you a huge debt of gratitude. You rescued my daughter, not once, but twice, from the wicked clutches of that tyrant! You risked your life to save her. To think what might have happened without your bravery!"

"Anyone in my position would've done the same, your Majesty," Josef said, modestly.

"I don't think so, Josef," replied the Queen, smiling, "Pitching your wits and knowledge against the might of Torrian and his hooligan horsemen, shows rare courage indeed."

"Thank you, your Majesty," Josef said quietly.

"What can I give you, then, as a gesture of my deep gratitude?" the Queen then asked.

Josef glanced down at his boots momentarily, and then said nervously, "There is really nothing, your Majesty."

"Nothing!" said the Queen, surprised. "Then you're the first man I've met who wants nothing! There must be one thing, just one, that you want?"

"I – I hardly dare say it, your Majesty." Josef looked at his hands and saw that they were trembling slightly. The Queen took his hands in hers. They were warm and soft. The Queen smiled at him, and said gently, "It's my daughter, isn't it? It's Emelia. You love her, don't you? And she loves you."

Josef tried to say something, but couldn't speak.

"It's alright Josef!" the queen said, squeezing his hands, "She's so lucky to have you! You have rare qualities indeed!"

"But I thought -" Josef began.

"Thought what, Josef? Perhaps as I did. Before I met you, that is. That a suitable husband must be rich and powerful? We have wealth and power enough in this family! But you must understand that wisdom, knowledge, courage, and yes, love, are all so much more important than material wealth. You'll make her a worthy husband, Josef. So marry her!"

There was a sudden knock at the door, and a servant appeared. Clearing his throat, he said, "I'm sorry to intrude your Majesty, but the King has requested that you and Master Josef come to the State Room."

"You go on ahead, Josef," said the Queen softly, "I'll be along in a minute."

Josef met Emelia just outside the State Room. When he told her of the conversation he'd just had with the Queen, she threw her arms around his neck and kissed him. She hugged him tightly and said joyfully, "Oh Josef! That's wonderful! So we can marry!"

She then pulled away a little, looked into his eyes, and smiled. "That's of course, if you were to ask me."

"*Will* you marry me, Princess Emelia?" said Josef, without delay.

"Last night I tried my hardest to imagine *not* marrying you! But I couldn't. I have to be with you, Josef. I have to!"

They hugged tightly. Just then the State Room door opened, and the King appeared.

"Good grief!" he blustered, "What's all this? Canoodling in my palace! I'm not sure we can have that!" He smiled, and then winked at them. "Come on in. We have important state business to attend to. Smooching can wait!"

King Otto sat in his throne, and gestured for Josef to come before him. Then he said, "It's been a long time since I had to do this, so please bear with me. Josef, your country, and the Kingdom of Maduria, both owe you their deep gratitude. Single-handedly you've not only rescued Princess Emelia twice, but in so doing have averted war between the countries. If that weren't enough, you've also foiled a plot to overthrow me as King! There is only one honour I can bestow upon you, that befits your actions. Zumbovias' highest! Please kneel."

Humbled, Josef knelt before the King, who stood, and drew out his sword. Tapping Josef on each shoulder, he said, "I pronounce you Knight of the Kingdom of Zumbovia. Arise, Sir Josef!"

Chapter Seventeen:
Happily Ever After

Emelia and Josef, or Sir Josef as we should now call him, stayed in Zumborg until the Grand Court Hearing. They were both expected to give evidence. There was also much to prepare for the wedding, and fortunately Queen Helena threw herself into organising it, leaving Josef and the Princess with plenty of time for long country walks.

When the Hearing convened, Zumbovias' twelve most senior judges were unanimous in their verdict, and both prisoners were found guilty of Conspiring to Overthrow the Monarchy. Torrian was also found guilty of Kidnapping.

The wedding took place a week later, and it was a wonderful occasion. Emelia looked stunning in a long, flowing white dress of purest silk, and Josef felt a little uncomfortable and self-conscious in the Zumbovian national costume, a kilt and jacket. There was a parade through the streets of Zumborg, and it seemed that everyone in both Kingdoms had crammed into the city for the day. In the evening there was music and dancing, and a sumptuous feast. Much later on, as Sir Josef and Princess Emelia watched a spectacular firework display, arm-in-arm, they looked at each other and knew that they would be happy together for the rest of their lives.

So at this point, we could easily say that they both lived happily ever after, and that would be the end of it. Yes? But perhaps you want to know what *really* happened to these people? What did they do for the rest of their lives?

Torrian was sentenced to slavery in Zumbovias' largest, deepest mine, where he was made to dig coal until he was an old man. He was released on his 60th birthday, and with some modest savings he'd made from the meagre stipend that slaves were paid, he purchased a small farm, on which he grew and ate vegetables and fruit for twenty years, until he died.

The Duke was sent to the State Prison, where he was appointed Chief Lavatory Attendant, although in truth he was forced to do all the really dirty, smelly jobs that nobody else wanted to do. After several years, he almost got to like it, and he even got used to the nick-name, *Pukey-Dukey*, that the other prisoners had given him.

With nobody living in it, Castle Suvorov soon fell into disrepair. Sophie, the maid who had bravely helped the Princess to escape from it, now found herself without work. Emelia asked her if she would consider becoming Personal Assistant to the Princess, a position of great responsibility, and one that Sophie delightedly accepted. In so doing, she found herself working closely with Johnson, and before long the two of them fell in love. They married, and had two children, a son they named Joe, and Emily, a delightful and cheeky little daughter who ran around the palace as if it were her own.

Sophies' brother Ivan decided to sell his cottage, and used the money to fulfil his dream to travel the world. After six years he returned from a country called India, a place that had clearly impressed him. He had long hair, and said the word "cool" a lot. He made an attempt to settle back down into life in Zumbovia, broke a few hearts, and then one day he suddenly announced that he had to travel again. The last anyone heard of him was that he'd become a Buddhist monk, far away in a kingdom called Bhutan.

Queen Helena returned to Madovar, and both she and King Otto resumed their duties as Heads of State. But the two monarchs had grown fond of each other, and visited each other often.

Sir Josef and Princess Emelia had four children, two boisterous sons, and two delightful daughters. Josef designed a wonderful new palace, and had it built entirely of wood, high up in The Pinnacles. It resembled a series of huge round-houses cascading one over the other, down into the steep-sided valley where he and Emelia had first kissed. She adored it, and they lived there in happiness, until they were very old.

The End

N.Stevenson
1st – 16th November 2004

Printed in Great Britain
by Amazon